Pop Corn and Ma Goodness

Pop Corn & Ma Goodness

Edna Mitchell Preston   Illustrated by Robert Andrew Parker

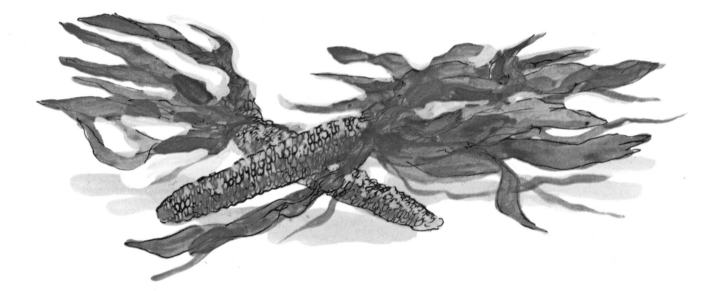

THE VIKING PRESS   NEW YORK

Text copyright © 1969 by Edna Mitchell Preston. Illustrations copyright © 1969 by Robert Andrew Parker. All rights reserved. First published in 1969 by The Viking Press, Inc., 625 Madison Avenue, New York, N.Y. 10022. Published simultaneously in Canada by The Macmillan Company of Canada Limited. Library of Congress catalog card number: 71-85864. Printed in U.S.A.

Pic Bk   1. Nonsense stories

Trade 670–56499–0   VLB 670–56500–8

Ma Goodness she's coming a-skippitty skoppetty

skippitty skoppetty

skippitty skoppetty

Ma Goodness she's coming a-skippitty skoppetty

All doon the hill.

Pop Corn he's a-coming a-hippitty hoppetty

hippitty hoppetty

hippitty hoppetty

Pop Corn he's a-coming a-hippitty hoppetty

All doon the hill.

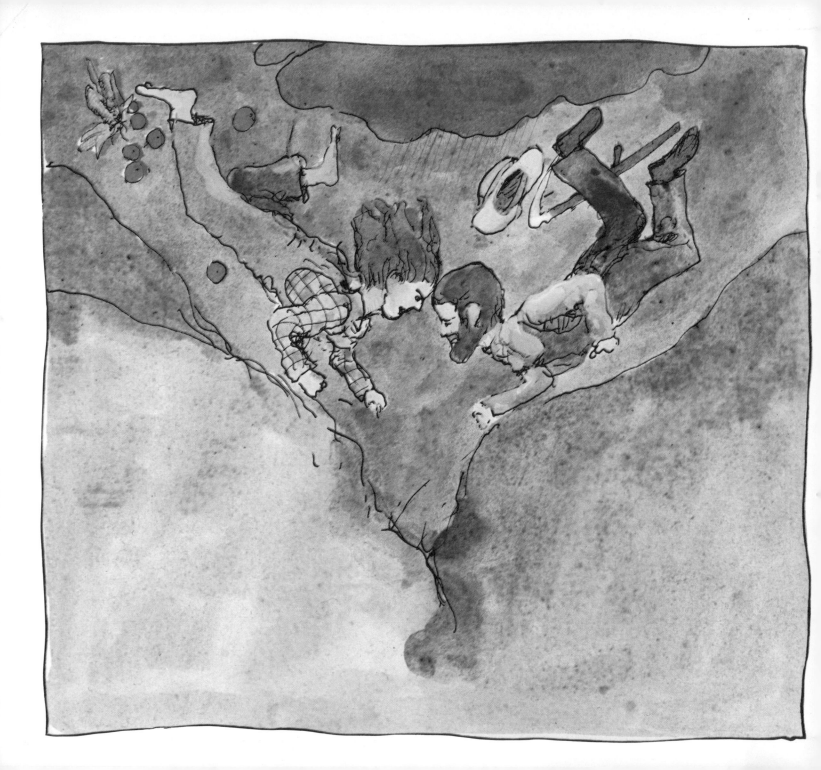

The rain it starts coming a-drippitty droppetty

The lane it gets slippitty slippitty sloppetty

Old Ma goes a-flying a-flippitty floppetty

Old Pop takes a header a-dippitty doppetty

They meet—oh their heads crack a-bippitty boppetty

    All doon the hill.

Old Ma she sees stars go a-skippitty skoppetty
"He loves me," she says, heart a-flippitty floppetty.

Old Pop's brains are addled and dippitty doppetty
"She loves me," he says, heart a-hippitty hoppetty.

They cotch them a horse, go a-clippitty cloppetty

The preacher he weds them a-lippitty loppetty

They build them a house all a-chippitty choppetty
They make them a farm all a-tippitty toppetty.

They make them a farm all a-tippitty toppetty
    All doon the hill.
They get them a goat, goes gallippitty galloppetty
    All doon the hill.

Old b'ar comes a-cropping a-crippitty croppetty
　　All doon the hill.
Old goat—oh the b'ar swots him bippitty boppetty
　　All doon the hill.

They give him a funeral—cry drippitty droppetty

    All doon the hill.

Pop gives that old b'ar his come-uppitty-oppetty

    All doon the hill.

They get them a hounddog, goes yippitty yippitty

yippitty yippitty

yippitty yippitty

They get them a hounddog, goes yippitty yippitty

All doon the hill.

They get them some kids for to whuppitty whoppetty

whuppitty whoppetty

whuppitty whoppetty

They get them some kids for to whuppitty whoppetty

All doon the hill.

Now Pop he chops firewood a-chippitty choppetty

And Ma redds the house up a-mippitty moppetty

The kids—oh they're brats all a-snippitty snoppetty

They whup one another a-bippitty boppetty

Old hounddog—they chase him a-yippitty yoppetty

     All doon the hill.

Come snowtime they all go a-flippitty floppetty

Up hill and doon a-plippitty ploppetty

Come springtime they all go a-trippitty troppetty

Up hill and doon on their prippitty proppetty.

A-chippitty choppetty

Mippitty moppetty

Snippitty snoppetty

Bippitty boppetty

Yippitty yoppetty

Flippitty floppetty

Together they go all a-lippitty loppetty

Up hill and doon on the dippitty doppetty

Tippitty toppetty prippitty proppetty

Of skippitty skoppetty hippitty hoppetty

POP CORN AND MA GOODNESS